This book
belongs to:

_____

For Lara Hancock and Tiffany Leeson who sent Sir Charlie off on his adventures,
and Alice Corrie and Sue Mason who brought him safely home.
K.S.

*Sir Charlie Stinky Socks would like to donate 10% of the royalties from
the sale of this book to Naomi House Children's Hospice.*

EGMONT
We bring stories to life

First published in Great Britain in 2017
by Egmont UK Limited
The Yellow Building, 1 Nicholas Road, London W11 4AN
www.egmont.co.uk

Text and illustrations copyright © Kristina Stephenson 2017

Kristina Stephenson has asserted her moral rights.

ISBN (HB) 978 14052 68110
ISBN (PB) 978 14052 68127

A CIP catalogue record for this book is available from the British Library.

THE DINOSAUR'S RETURN

Kristina Stephenson

EGMONT

Once upon a moonlit night

in a **MUSEUM OF MARVELLOUS THINGS** —
high on a shelf, where a cat was sleeping,
something began to stir . . .

You see, amongst the *treasures* and *trinkets* on the shelf
there was a most **unusual egg**,
and the cat's warm fur and gentle purr
were waking whatever was inside it.

Tippety-tap,
tippety-tap
the shell began to crack.

And out came the strangest
little something
the cat had ever seen.

Oh my!

How fortunate then that
Sir Charlie Stinky Socks
was studying maps in the MUSEUM that night
and heard his cat, Envelope, calling,

"Meeeeeeooow!"

Map in hand he bounded over
to help his faithful friend.

"*Jinkies!*" said Sir Charlie
when he saw the **little something**.

Whatever could it be?

Unknown
Egg
Found at the foot of
Thunder Mountain,
in the middle of the
big, blue sea.

"I don't know what this
little something is," he said,
"but we need to take it home."

Thunder Mountain
was on the map, so Sir
Charlie charted a course.

He polished his **sword**
and pocketed some **string**
(which he'd kept from
his last adventure).

And with a
rallying
cry of

"*to Thunder Mountain!*"

he mounted his good grey mare.

Clip-clop   clip-clop
clippety,   clippety,   clop

down to the harbour to borrow a boat from a **pirate** Sir Charlie knew.

"I promise to bring back your boat,"
called Sir Charlie as he headed for the horizon.

Sir Charlie and his friends sailed through the night
by the light of a silvery moon, and by morning,
they'd reached the spot on the map
where the *Mountain* was meant to be.

But where was *Thunder Mountain*?
All they could see was . . .

. . . sea.

They searched the island for signs of life,
but they didn't have any luck.

So they climbed to the top of the
Mountain to see what
they could see.

But the ground was **shaking**.
The cat was **quaking**.
And poor old Envelope *slipped*.

Oh no!

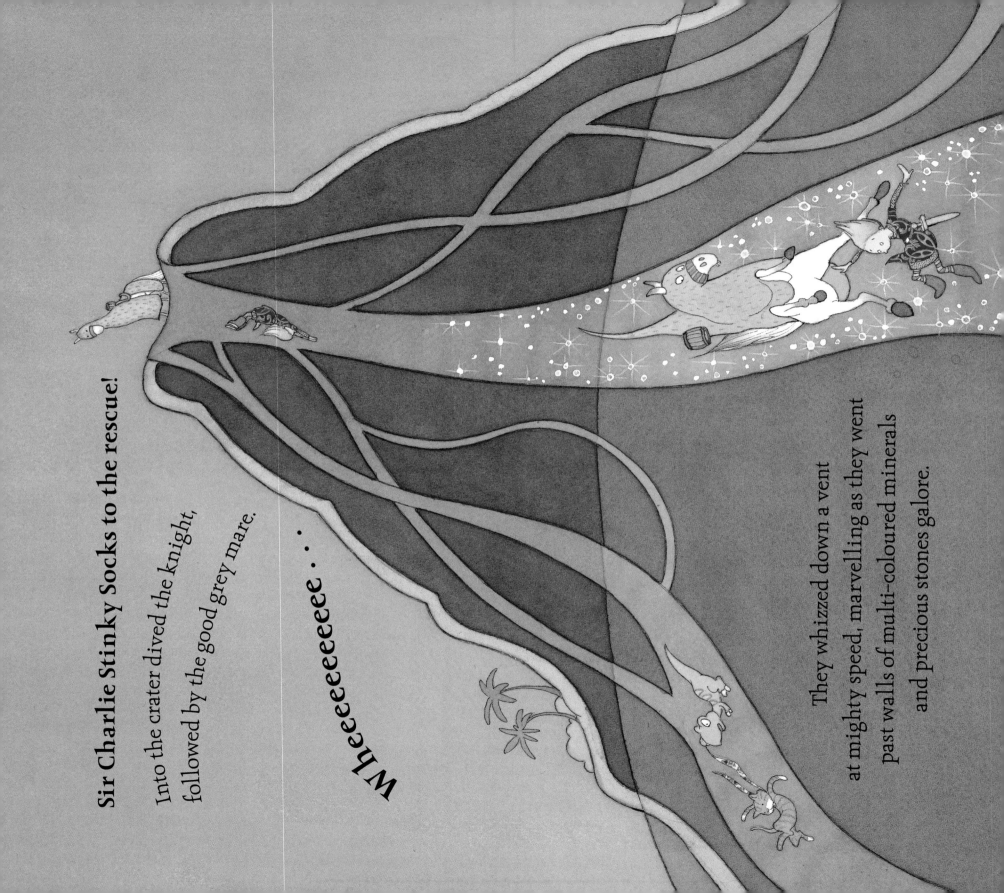

Sir Charlie Stinky Socks to the rescue!

Into the crater dived the knight,
followed by the good grey mare.

Wheeeeeeeee . . .

They whizzed down a vent
at mighty speed, marvelling as they went
past walls of multi-coloured minerals
and precious stones galore.

Luckily, they landed softly at the bottom, in a chamber full of ash.

"Hooray and hurrah!" said Sir Charlie. "There isn't any lava. *Thunder Mountain* will **NEVER** erupt."

But . . . .

. . . **Envelope wasn't there. Oh my! "He's LOST!"** gasped the worried knight. "We **have** to go and find him."

They hurried out of the dusty chamber . . .

But didn't get very far . . .

"*Yikes!*" said Sir Charlie to his terrified horse, as they teetered on the brink. "And I think we've **shrunk**," he said when he realised that everything else was **ENORMOUS!**

Just then Sir Charlie spotted Envelope, way off in the distance, with the **little something** (who'd grown much bigger) trotting along behind.

And there was Envelope just below.
"Tally ho!" cried the knight.

"Time to jump,"
said Sir Charlie,
spotting a **crystal pool**.

"On my count," he said to the horse.

**"One,
two,
three . . ."**

Splash!

"Perfect landing!" said Sir Charlie.

Except . . .

. . . the gulping, grey mare **couldn't swim.**

"*Phew!*" huffed the knight as he heaved his horse onto a nearby island.

"And Envelope can't be very far away. Why don't I use the smell from my stockings to let him know we're here?"

Sir Charlie wafted his socks in the air and waited to see what would happen.

But before he could tell if his plan had worked, the **pool** began to **bubble** . . .

"Uh oh! We're in trouble," said Sir Charlie, as . . .

The island lifted its head.